Put Beginning Readers on the Righ
ALL ABOARD READING

The All Aboard Reading series is especial _____ _ginning readers. Written by noted authors and illustrated in full color, these are books that children really and truly *want* to read—books to excite their imagination, tickle their funny bone, expand their interests, and support their feelings. With four different reading levels, All Aboard Reading lets you choose which books are most appropriate for your children and their growing abilities.

Picture Readers—for Ages 3 to 6
Picture Readers have super-simple texts with many nouns appearing as rebus pictures. At the end of each book are 24 flash cards—on one side is the rebus picture; on the other side is the written-out word.

Level 1—for Preschool through First Grade Children
Level 1 books have very few lines per page, very large type, easy words, lots of repetition, and pictures with visual "cues" to help children figure out the words on the page.

Level 2—for First Grade to Third Grade Children
Level 2 books are printed in slightly smaller type than Level 1 books. The stories are more complex, but there is still lots of repetition in the text and many pictures. The sentences are quite simple and are broken up into short lines to make reading easier.

Level 3—for Second Grade through Third Grade Children
Level 3 books have considerably longer texts, use harder words and more complicated sentences.

All Aboard for happy reading!

For Mom and Dad—L.D.

Even the cats are brave in Brooklyn—D.D.R.

Photo p. 32, AP/Wide World Photos

Text copyright © 1997 by Laura Driscoll. Illustrations copyright © 1997 by DyAnne DiSalvo-Ryan. All rights reserved. Published by Grosset & Dunlap, Inc., a member of The Putnam & Grosset Group, New York. ALL ABOARD READING is a trademark of The Putnam & Grosset Group. GROSSET & DUNLAP is a trademark of Grosset & Dunlap, Inc. Published simultaneously in Canada. Printed in the U.S.A.

Library of Congress Cataloging-in-Publication Data
Driscoll, Laura.
    The bravest cat! : the true story of Scarlett / by Laura Driscoll : illustrated by DyAnne DiSalvo-Ryan.
        p.   cm.—(All aboard reading. Level 1)
    Summary: The true story of a mother cat that becomes a celebrity when she rescues her kittens from a burning building in New York in 1996.
    1. Scarlett (Cat)—Juvenile literature. 2. Wellen, Karen—Juvenile literature. 3. Cats—New York (State)—New York—Biography—Juvenile literature. [1. Scarlett (Cat) 2. Cats.]
I. DiSalvo-Ryan, DyAnne, ill. II. Title. III. Series.
SF445.7.D75   1997
636.8'092'9—dc21   97-10487
                                                                                                       CIP
                                                                                                        AC

ISBN 0-448-41720-0 (GB)   A B C D E F G H I J

ISBN 0-448-41703-0 (pbk.) A B C D E F G H I J

ALL
ABOARD
READING™
Level 1
Preschool-Grade 1

The Bravest CAT!

The True Story of Scarlett

By Laura Driscoll
Illustrated by DyAnne DiSalvo-Ryan

Grosset & Dunlap • New York

Brooklyn, NY, 1996

A building is on fire!
There are lots of fire engines
and lots of firemen.
It is a big fire
in an old garage.
But one thing is lucky.
No one lives in the building.

Wait! Look!

What do the firemen see?

It is a cat!
She runs out of the garage.

She is carrying something—
something small.
It is a tiny kitten!

The cat puts her kitten
in a safe place.

Then she runs back into the fire!
What is she doing?

Soon the cat runs out again—
with another kitten!

She runs in and out

three more times.

The firemen cannot
believe their eyes.
Now there is a pile of kittens!

They are tiny and scared.
One has burns on his little ears.

And the poor mother cat!

Her burns are bad.

Her eyes are hurt.

She cannot even

see her kittens.

So she touches each kitten

with her nose.

One, two, three, four, five.

They are all there.

Very gently,

a fireman puts

all of the cats into a box.

He can tell

they need a doctor.

The fireman takes the cats
to the animal hospital.

The cats do not belong to anyone.

They are strays.

So the doctors
give the mother cat a name.

They call her Scarlett
because of her red burns.

Soon lots of people
know about Scarlett.
Newspapers run stories.

People want her to be on TV.

She is a hero and a star.

Everyone hopes
Scarlett will get better.
And slowly she does.
The kittens are kept
in another room
so she can rest.
Scarlett cannot take care
of them anymore.

The people at the hospital
give the kittens lots of love.
And they get better, too—
all except one.

The doctors think
he was the last kitten
to get out of the fire.
The smoke hurt his lungs.
A month later,
he dies.

But the other kittens
get new homes.
Two kittens go home
with a woman.

The other two go home
with a couple from Long Island.

And what about Scarlett?
Letters for her come
from all over the world—
from Canada,
Japan, and even Egypt!
So many people
want to give her a good home.

The people at the hospital
read more than 1,000 letters!
They try to find
the best home for Scarlett.

At last,

they make up their minds.

TV and newspaper reporters

come to hear the big news.

A woman named Karen Wellen
will care for Scarlett.

In her letter, Karen wrote
about her own accident—
a car accident.

Like Scarlett,
it took a long time
for Karen to get better.
She knows what Scarlett
has been through.

Karen also had a cat before.
She loved it a lot.

But Karen's cat died
just after her accident.

Karen did not want
to get another cat—
unless it was a very special one…

just like Scarlett!